by Roger Hargreaves

Little Miss Brainy was very brainy.

She knew an awful lot of things.

She knew simple things such as
if you want a good night's sleep you
have to go to bed.

And, if you want to get up,
then first, you have to wake up.

She knew that if you don't want to be hungry,
you have to eat.

Little Miss Brainy
also knew lots of very clever things.

She knew that it is quite impossible
for centipedes to find matching coloured
shoes for **all** their feet.

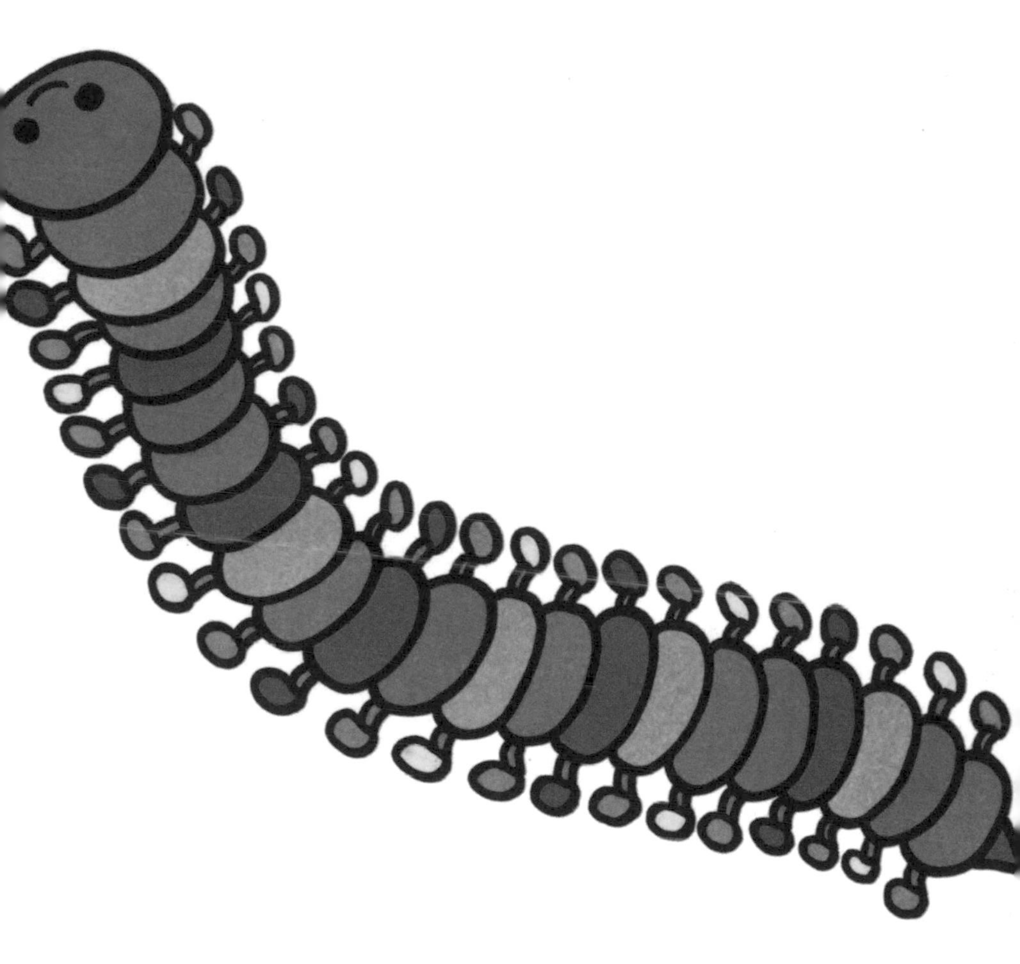

Now, Little Miss Brainy knew so much
that people got to hear about it.

They came from far and wide
to ask her questions.

Mr Messy called to see her.

“What can I do to keep myself messy?”
he asked.

“I know!” cried Little Miss Brainy.
“Don’t wash!”

Mr Messy was delighted.

As Mr Messy was leaving, Mr Dizzy arrived.

“Is there anything heavier than a hippopotamus?” asked Mr Dizzy.

“I know!” said Little Miss Brainy. “Two hippopotamuses!”

“Is that so?” said Mr Dizzy. “I’ll go and check.”

Mr Clever arrived.
"What colour is my green hat?" he asked.

"I know!" sighed Little Miss Brainy,
nodding her head.
"It's green, of course!"

"Oh, you know so many clever things!"
exclaimed Mr Clever.

Mr Clever left,
and so did Little Miss Brainy.

She had had enough of listening to
such simple questions.

So she travelled to a place called Cleverland,
where she hoped that everybody would ask
her some difficult questions for a change.

When she got there, she stopped
in front of a tree.

There was a pig sitting on one of its branches.

“However am I going to get down from here?”
wailed the pig.

“I know!” said Little Miss Brainy.
“You can jump down!”

“Good idea,” said the pig,
and being a Cleverland pig he jumped...
right on top of Little Miss Brainy.

“You’re not as soft a a pillow,”
he complained, and he trotted off.

Further down the road
Little Miss Brainy met an elephant.

He had a knot tied in his trunk.

“Please ’elp be. How cad I ud-do dis dot id by trunk?” he asked, in a funny sort of way.

“I know,” said Little Miss Brainy.
“I’ll undo it for you.”

And she did.

“Phew!” gasped the elephant.

And blew Little Miss Brainy high into the air!

“I feel much better now,” said the elephant.

“I don’t!” moaned Little Miss Brainy,
and rubbed her head.

The elephant had blown her some
distance away and she landed in front of a...

...lion!

“I’m starving!” growled the lion.
“What can I eat?”

Little Miss Brainy looked around,
but she could see nothing,
and said quickly...

“I don’t know!”

And she ran home,
before the lion realised
that she was the only
thing to eat for miles around!

cut along the dotted line and return this whole page

Fantastic offers for Little Miss fans!

Collect all your Mr. Men or Little Miss books in these superb durable collectors' cases!
Only £5.99 inc. postage and packing, these wipe-clean, hard-wearing cases will give all your Mr. Men or Little Miss books a beautiful new home!

Keep track of your collection with this giant-sized double-sided Mr. Men and Little Miss Collectors' poster.
Collect 6 tokens and we will send you a brilliant giant-sized double-sided collectors' poster! Simply tape a £1 coin to cover postage and packaging in the space provided and fill out the form overleaf.

STICK £1 COIN HERE
(for poster only)

Only need a few Little Miss or Mr. Men to complete your set? You can order any of the titles on the back of the books from our Mr. Men order line on 0870 787 1724. Orders should be delivered between 5 and 7 working days.

TO BE COMPLETED BY AN ADULT

To apply for any of these great offers, ask an adult to complete the details below and send this whole page with the appropriate payment and tokens, to: MR. MEN CLASSIC OFFER, PO BOX 715, HORSHAM RH12 5WG

☐ Please send me a giant-sized double-sided collectors' poster.

AND ☐ I enclose 6 tokens and have taped a £1 coin to the other side of this page.

☐ Please send me ☐ Mr. Men Library case(s) and/or ☐ Little Miss library case(s) at £5.99 each inc P&P

☐ I enclose a cheque/postal order payable to Egmont UK Limited for £..........

OR ☐ Please debit my MasterCard / Visa / Maestro / Delta account (delete as appropriate) for £..........

Card no. ☐☐☐☐☐☐☐☐☐☐☐☐☐☐☐☐☐☐☐ Security code ☐☐☐

Issue no. (if available) ☐ Start Date ☐☐/☐☐/☐☐ Expiry Date ☐☐/☐☐/☐☐

Fan's name: .... Date of birth: ....

Address: ....

....

.... Postcode: ....

Name of parent / guardian: ....

Email for parent / guardian: ....

Signature of parent / guardian: ....

Please allow 28 days for delivery. Offer is only available while stocks last. We reserve the right to change the terms of this offer at any time and we offer a 14 day money back guarantee. This does not affect your statutory rights. Offers apply to UK only.

☐ We may occasionally wish to send you information about other Egmont children's books. If you would rather we didn't, please tick this box.

Ref: LIM 001

cut along the dotted line and return this whole page